AF333107

My Underwear's Inside Out!

THE CARE AND FEEDING OF YOUNGER POETS

Diane Dawber

ILLUSTRATED BY
Pat Wilkinson

PREFACE BY
David Booth

QUARRY PRESS

to Chris, the M's and the K's

CONTENTS

Preface

I have been reading Diane Dawber's poems for a long time, and this new book, *My Underwear's Inside Out*, is a wonderful addition to her successful collection.

Diane has a talent for making poetry come to life, so that as we read a poem we catch a glimpse of what she wants us to see, and suddenly we feel what she hopes we will feel. It's quite amazing how so few words on a page can trigger so much meaning in us. But that is the secret of poetry, condensed like frozen orange juice, and we must add the rest.

I first met Diane at a conference when she was helping teachers learn more about using poems with children, and I was so impressed with her quiet, persuasive manner. Then, when I read her words, her voice seemed to enter each poem, and I realized how important it is for the poet's life to be part of everything she writes. We must begin with ourselves—what we see and hear, what we remember, what we think about, what we dream of. These will be the poems that matter to others and to ourselves, and in this book, Diane Dawber will take you by the hand and lead you on a journey into the world of poetry, and you will experience both this poet's talents as well as your own excitement at poetic writing.

This poet knows all the techniques: she will help you make words swirl around the page, paint magic pictures with only words to work with, find ways of describing events by using exploding comparisons, and demonstrate how to tell complete stories with the economy of a poem.

Diane Dawber is a wordsmith, crafting her poems from ribbons of thought, and we can read and share her creations and gain courage to try our own. She knows a great deal about the care and feeding of younger poets, and you are about to benefit from her love of poetry. I hope your underwear isn't inside out!

David Booth

Foreword

I wasn't thinking of vaccinations against measles or peanut butter sandwiches when I gave this book the subtitle "The Care and Feeding of Younger Poets." Younger poets do need these things, but they also need words to play with, stories to act out, and tender listening care from parents and teachers to encourage their reading and writing.

We all need to play more. Why? When we play, we take what we know and put it together in different ways. We find out what works and what doesn't. We discover new things. If we play with sand and water, we learn more about sand and water. We also make mud. And when we play with words and experiences, we not only learn more about these things, we create something new—poetry.

How? Read these poems to your child and let your child read the poems to you. Read them together like miniature plays, in all kinds of voices, serious and funny. Ham it up! Tell your child stories that come to mind as you read and let your child tell you stories. And if the younger poets in your home or classroom are eager to write poetry, then read with them the simple instructions I've placed at the end of each section. You may find yourself writing poetry, too.

So, think of poetry as a wide beach, with grains of experience for sand and waves of words for water. Dig in and enjoy yourselves.

Diane Dawber

Into The Bear's Mouth

dump the pieces out of the box
turn them over
sort out the edges
assemble the frame
make piles of the same color
look at the box picture
and put together the bear's eye
then all his white fur
but the mouth is missing.

All the blue sky
all the blue-green water
all the blue-white ice
go together fine
but
the mouth's still missing so

I check
in the box
under the box
in my lap
under me
down the chair
and under the table
while accusing everyone near
of hiding that piece just to tease
but
the mouth's still missing.

I want to know
if the bear is smiling
or roaring
or snarling.
That blank space
makes the bear
yawn with possibilities.

Next day, putting my clothes in the laundry
something drops from a crease.
I race to the puzzle and fit that
mouthful of fish
into place with a sigh.

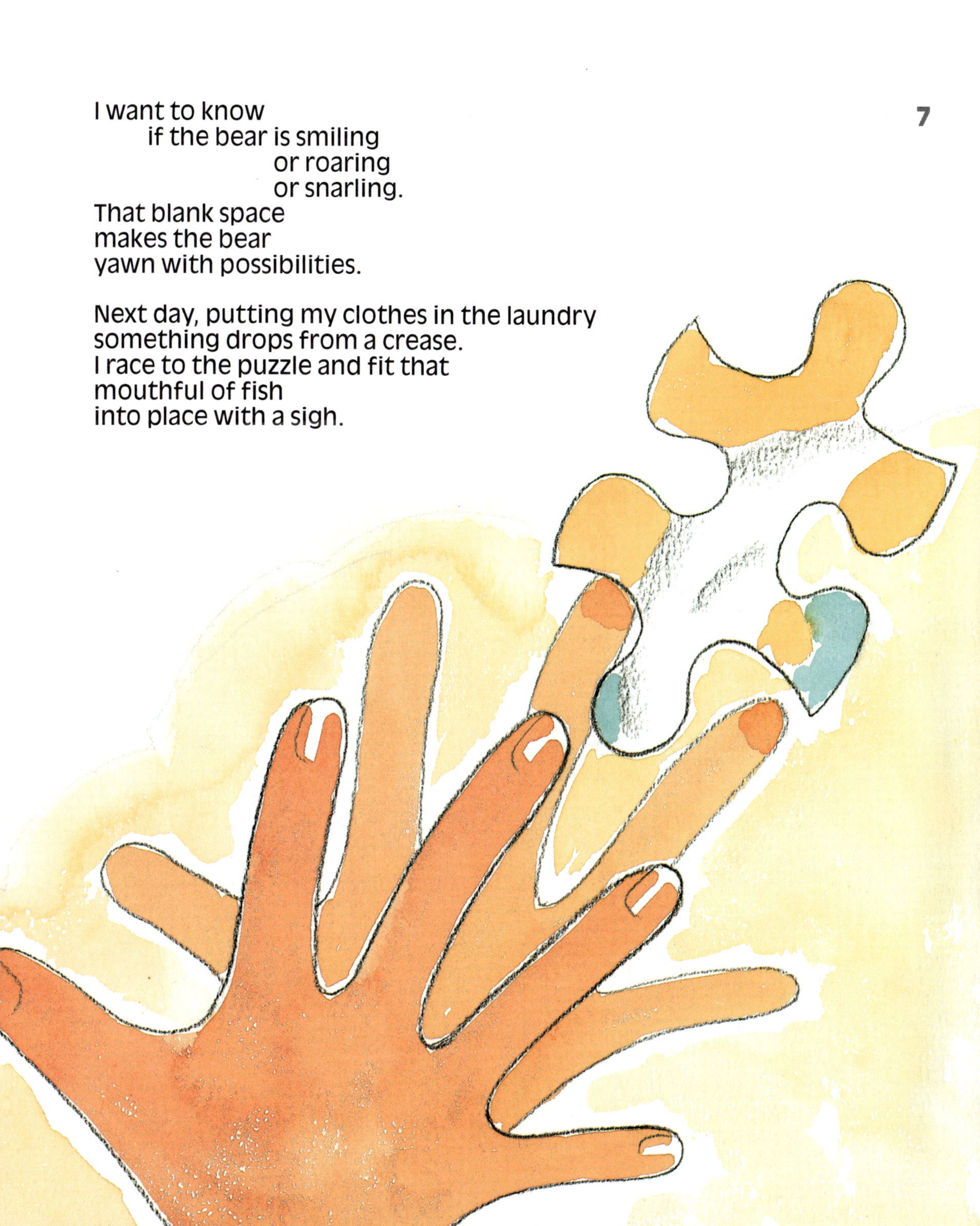

1
King Crayfish And Other Human Video Poems

King Crayfish

"Look at this," said Rosemary
as she showed us
her giant crayfish in a jar.
It was grayish brown
with one big pincer and one small.
It clacked against the sides of the jar.
"Those stalks with the black things
are its eyes!
This must be the King of all crayfish."

So we all went
down to the creek
to flip over stones
scoop with bottles
capture our own crayfish
bigger
we hoped
than Rosemary's.

Some of us were wading
but I was too afraid
bent over the bank and

FELL IN.

THE KING CRAYFISH
AND HIS ARMY
ALL POINTED THEIR PINCERS STRAIGHT AT ME
AND I COULD FEEL THEM NIPPING
AS I RAN
WET AND HOWLING

H-O-O-o-o-m-e.

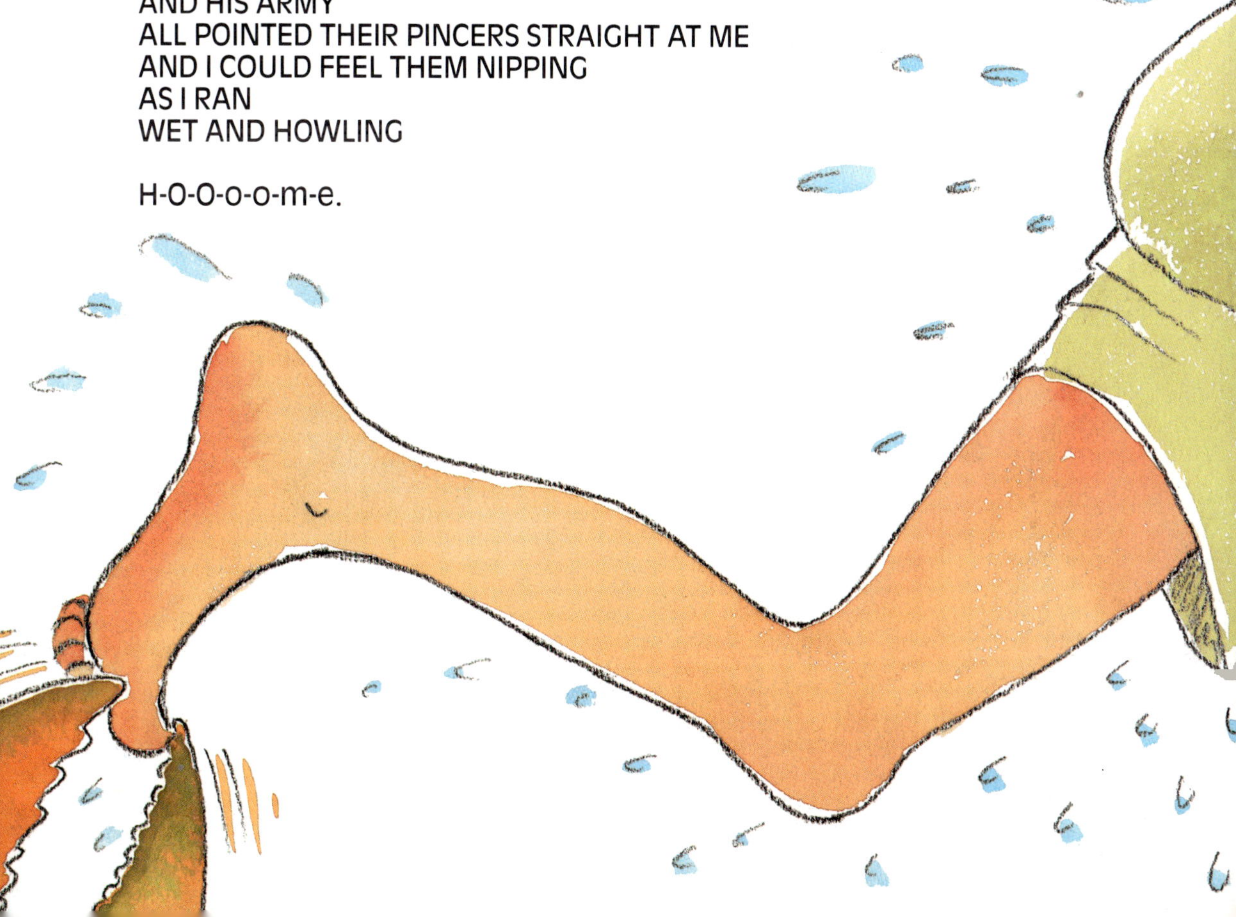

My Tongue Is Orange

Down in the freezer
on a summer day
there's maybe a chocolate
a lime or a cherry
banana or for sure
orange, gummy
frozen to its bag or
just frosty right.

If you hold it like fingers
crack it on the counter edge
you can share the drips
trickling over your hand
cleaning a path down your arm
and spotting your feet
where the last chunk lands
speckled in the dirt.

Suck the wood and
save it for your collection of
POPSICLE STICKS.

Get Your Ice Cold News Here!

See the dentist.
See the doc.
Pick up your sister at four o'clock.

Milk and bread
and mow the lawn.
See if the garbage truck has already gone.

Read one old report card,
and two cartoons up top.
Now open up the coldness and have a pop.

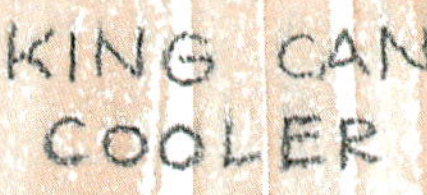

Winter Trails

Hoop and point
            long double lines
SKIER!

Split toes in a row
DEER!

Paws
with nails
DOG!

Furry
toes
CAT!

Long-tailed
            skiiiiiid
SQUIRREL!

Subways
        in
          the
            grass
MICE!

Waffles
            and grids
ME!

So much company and I didn't see a soul.

'Sno Go

Past my math book
past the teacher
past the curtains
past the window

I can see the first flakes
first white against the grey sky
first white against brown trees
first white against black pavement.

In one minute I can go
melt them on my tongue
watch them on my sleeve
throw them in faces.

There's the bell!
Please let us go!
Row by row, sure.
Quietly even!

"Before teachers dismiss classes, there is one announcement. Because many have not worn the proper clothing for snow recess will be INDOORS today."

ARRGGHH!

Bikes Need Bug Screens

Jean and I were walking
after supper
when
Jack rode past us fast.

Jean and I were swatting
at evening bugs
like caterpillars with wings
when
mouth open
in a silent whoop
Jack rode past us fast.

Jean and I were listening
when
just as he passed us.
Jack said, "Gack!"

Jean and I were giggling
when
Jack rode on fast
coughing and hacking.

IMPRESSIVE—
riding that fast
with a
bug in your stomach!

How To Ruin A Good Chew

Sick
in bed with red measles
my skin is dry
my body is red
my face is measled.
Can't read
because my eyes hurt.
Can't get up
because I'm dizzy
but
Dad brings bubblegum
cherry
wild cherry bubblegum
so I chew it
until my skin cools off
until my body goes pale
until my face loses its measles.
I can read again
Little Lulu comics
and fight with my sister
but
wild cherry bubblegum?
Ugh!

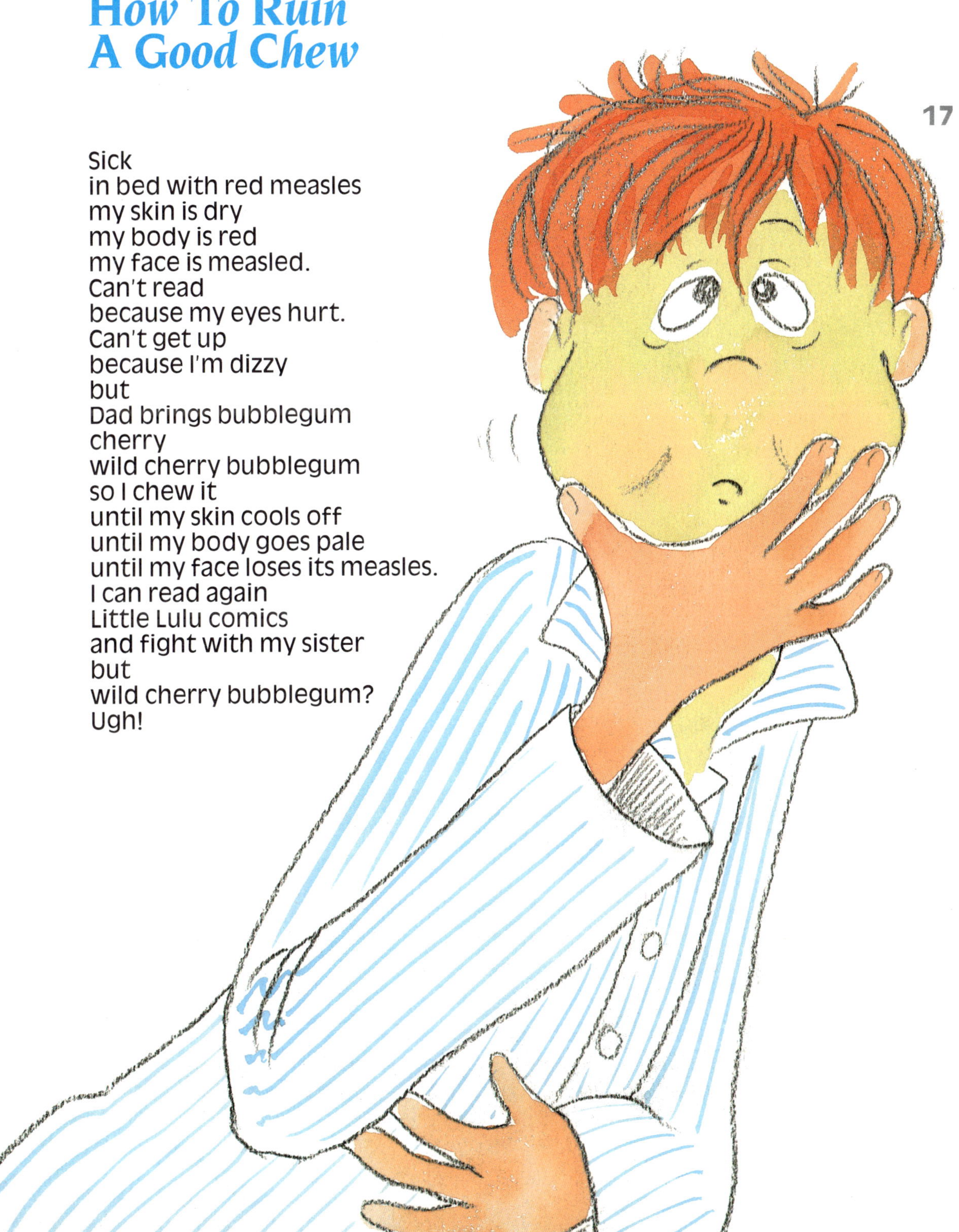

THE HUMAN VIDEO

When we close our eyes, most of us can still see a picture of our surroundings. When we remember something that happened to us, we can see a movie of it in our minds. Even when we pretend, we can see in our minds what we imagine. It's as if we each have our own mental camera. This camera can help us with our writing.

One way is to let the picture run as a movie and just describe what happens. Another way is to stop the picture and look carefully at everything in it and tell what you see. Either way you can zoom in for a close-up or zoom out for a wide shot. You can start from one side and move across or up and down. Of course, as your mental camera moves, you tell just what you see.

This can make a mystery. Imagine showing just parts of a shadowy room and then showing what lives there.

This can make an adventure. Imagine telling about each step as a rollercoaster gets to the top and then swoops down.

This can make a fright. Imagine giving sounds approaching in the dark and then illuminating what made them.

This can make a laugh. Imagine showing a bedroom and a lump under the covers and then a dog's head on the pillow snoring away.

My mental camera helped me write the poem *My Tongue Is Orange.* I made close-ups with my mental camera and I was careful not to show the popsicle. My camera followed my hand as it went into the freezer at the store where all the frozen treats are. My other hand opened the bag a bit so I could see what it was like and make sure it was the flavour I wanted. Then my hand whacked the treat on the edge of the counter. Then my hand took out one part and gave it to my friend. It took the other part and lifted it to my mouth. Some juice started to trickle down my hand, then down my arm. Now my camera follows the drops down to my feet and while it's down there a hunk falls in the dirt. Now the camera goes all the way back up to my mouth. The treat is all gone and my hand is holding the stick. I finally tell what I've been eating.

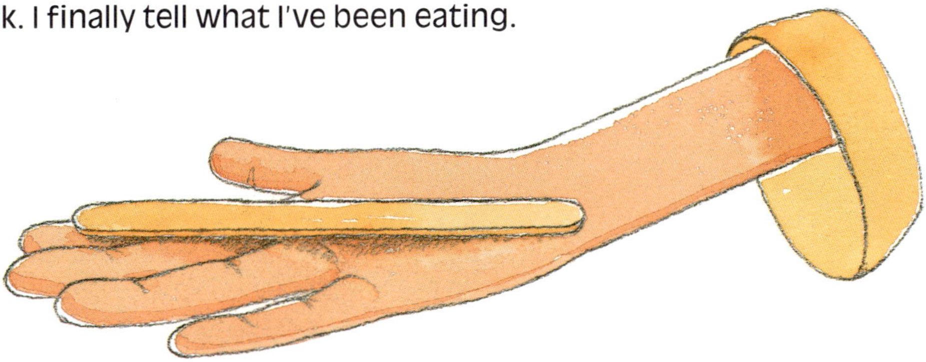

This is just like a small movie except that it's mostly silent. I left out what my friend and I said because I wanted to concentrate on the popsicle. It also makes the last line more startling because it is loud when I finally say what it is I've been eating.

King Crayfish uses different shots, too. First, the close-up of Rosemary and her crayfish in the jar; then a wide-angle of all of us; a close-up of me bending over the creek's bank and falling in; and, last, a long distance shot of me running home in a panic.

When you write a poem you can use all the tricks a camera can use. You can do close-ups. You can go way back. You can move up and down or side to side. You can keep something out of the picture until the last as a surprise or fright or laugh. You can turn the sound up or down to make it peaceful or scary. You can even hear what someone is thinking.

If you have an idea for a poem, try using your mental camera. Decide what your shots will be.

Decide what is the important thing in each shot. It might be a sound, a taste, a smell, a touch, a sight or a thought.

Now write the words that will tell someone about each shot.

When you have written your poem, you will probably want to try it out on someone. Try it on yourself first. Read it out loud. Change anything that your tongue stumbles over. Pay attention when your mouth uses a different word than your hand. Your mouth is the expert on talking unless you sign.

Now find someone who likes you and ask her or him to read it. Ask your person to tell you what he or she finds. That way you will know if your poem said what you thought it said. If it doesn't quite, you can change or add or take out things until it does. Or, you can try a different poem.

Have fun, video-brain!

2
Harmonica Howls And Other Sound-Track Poems

Harmonica Howls

"Let ME play it."

My sister grabs for my new shiny harmonica
which I'm breathing into
and sucking out
with a wonderful wheeze.

"NO.
I SAVED my money.
You SPENT yours on candy."

"Let me play it, PLEASE?"

"WELL
give me some of your candy."

"CAN'T.
It's all gone."

"TOO BAD.
Besides
I don't want YOUR germs all over MY harmonica."

"GIVE it to me!"

"No!" and I hold it up over my head
out of reach.

"I want a HARMONICA!"

I watch her as she wrinkles up her face.
She is going to cry.
What a crybaby!

"WAAH!
I want a harmonica!
I want a harmonica like HERS!"

I saved my allowance
I saved nickels
from pulling weeds
drying dishes
and watering the garden
for one
nickel-plated
dime store
harmonica
which I got today.

My sister
howled
for one
nickel-plated
dime-store
harmonica
which she got today.

I wouldn't have minded
listening to her howl.

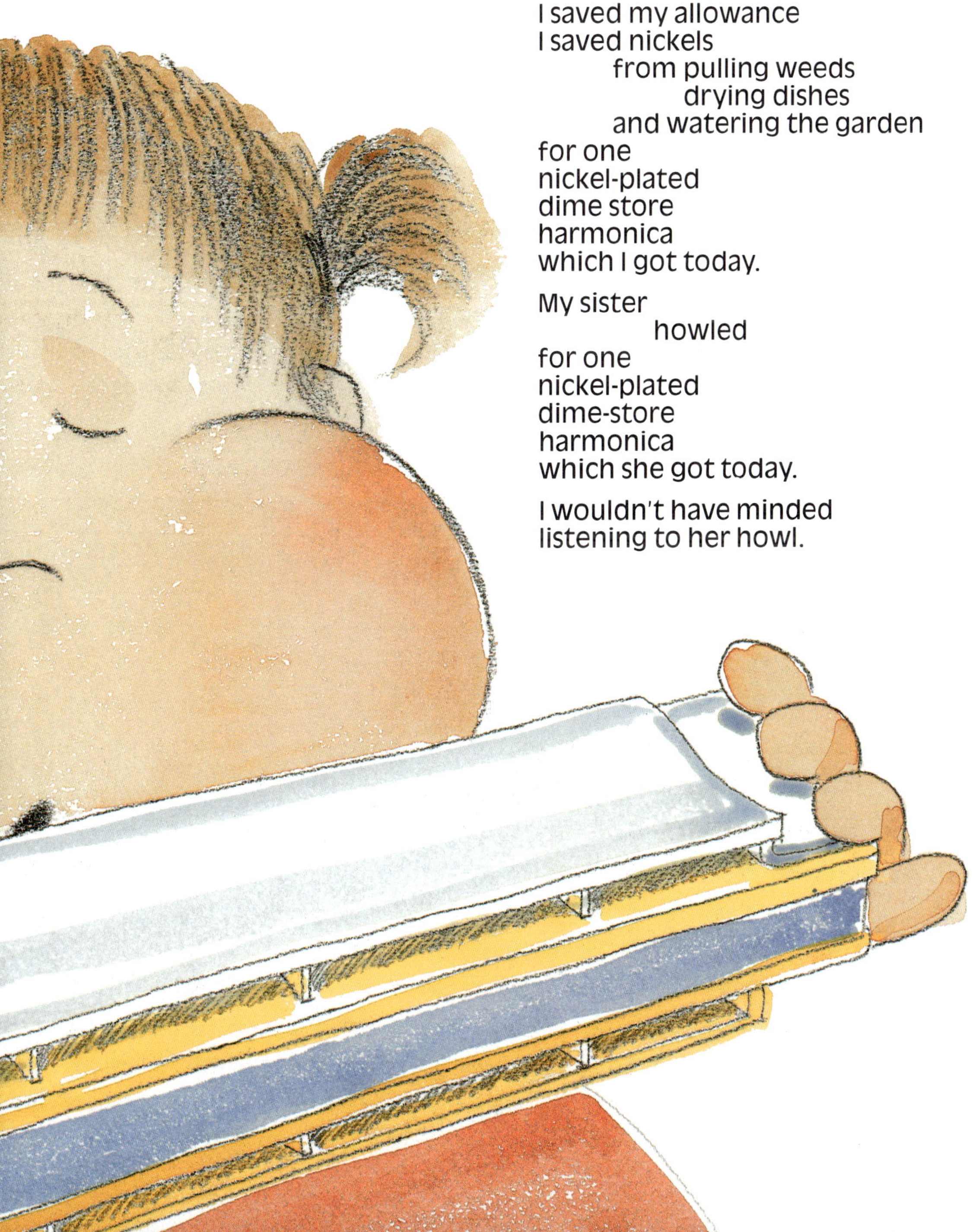

Forget I Mentioned It

I made a mistake
the first time I had a Braunschweiger
sandwich in my lunch.

My mistake was
I told my mother I liked it.

Every day now I get
Braunschweiger sandwiches in my lunch.

Every day now I throw
my Braunschweiger sandwich in the garbage.

Why don't I tell her
I am tired of it?

I can hear
"But you said you liked it.
Why don't you like it now?
Don't tell me you threw good food in the garbage!"

It is easier to do without lunch.

The Rattrays' Mailbox

One mailbox on the way home
has something missing
so it says:
"RAT RAY"

It makes me wonder:
Is there a rat named Ray living there?
What kind of rat has a mailbox?
Or gets letters?

"RAT RAY"

It makes me think:
If you open the box flap
will a transformer beam
shoot out and change me into a rat?
What mad scientist lives there?

"RAT RAY"

It makes me ask:
If the rats try to steal the mail
will they be exterminated?
Why would rats steal mail?
Can they read?

I'm going to keep an eye peeled
for deliveries.

Spinning The World

The dress is navy blue with brown trim
    but THAT isn't why I LIKE it.
Ugh! What ugly colors!

The dress is made of heavy knitted stuff
    but that isn't why I like it EITHER.
I wish it were silky.

BUT

the skirt is SO round
    you can TURN in a circle
        and it will TWIRL straight out.
    I can make myself DIZZY
whirling in a gypsy dance.

THAT'S
why I like it.

Shaking My Shadow

"Want to go to the pond?"

"Hey, yeah. That would be great."

My cousin is sixteen and she
takes me places
let's me do stuff with her.

"I wanna go too."

My sister wants to go too
but she gets halfway there
and cries to go home
cries to go to the bathroom
cries to do something else.

We run.

We climb onto the woodshed roof to hide
but she finds us.

"I see you. I see you. I want up."

We don't say anything.

"I SEE you. I SEE you.
I want UP."

We STILL don't say anything but
it is hard not to giggle.

"I SEE YOU. I SEE YOU.
I WANT UP."

WE STILL DON'T SAY ANYTHING.

"WAAH! I'LL TELL!"

My sister hollers and dances
whoops and stomps
and halfway to our giving in
she gives up
and wanders off after the cat.

I forget if we went anywhere
but I always wonder
if we were too mean.

Bug Juice

Tomato plants get caterpillars.
Caterpillars eat their leaves.
Then the tomato plants die.
So John has the job of
picking off caterpillars
and
with his workboots
STEPPING ON THEM.

They S-Q-U-E-L-C-H!

John is letting me help
pick off the caterpillars
so he can
STEP ON THEM.

They S-Q-U-E-L-C-H!

"Look at this one," he says.
"This is the biggest we've found."
He drops it in the dust
between the rows of tomato plants
and
STEPS ON IT.

"AARRGH!" I scream.
"You've splatted it all over me!
I've got bug guts all over me!"

"Ha!" he laughs.
"Aw!" he says.

Then he takes out his handkerchief
and tries to wipe me off
but I'm whirling around too much.
"I'm going home!" I scream
and I do.
I'll show him.
He can pick his own caterpillars.
He can splat them on himself.
I imagine John with bug guts all over him
which would be funny
except
I wouldn't be there to see.
Better go back.
I wouldn't want to miss anything.

Please Make A Joke

We were playing baseball
when Patsy got hit by a line drive.
I ran up with the rest
to where Patsy was holding her ankle.
Patsy was crying.
"Patsy," I said.
"You'll have to start wearing a glove on your ankle."
Her tears were so clear.
but she smiled through them
sort of like sunlight through drizzle
until the teacher came
to help her away.

We were skipping Double Dutch
when Andrea tripped and fell.
I crowded around with the rest
where Andrea was holding
her bloody, gravelly knee.
"Andrea," I said.
"You'll do anything to get out of Phys. Ed."
Before Andrea could smile
Muriel turned on me
"You've always got to make
a joke of everything!
Don't you care when somebody gets hurt?"

I turned away
                    away
                         away.
Please, somebody, make a joke.

Amnesia

I said my speech today.

It started
"Honorable judges
and fellow classmates."

It ended
"Thank you for listening."

Funny thing is
I can't remember what was in between
except that
Jimmy snickered
Sarah grinned
Jeremy shot some eraser
and it had something to do with gerbils.

Phone-A-Phobia

Go on now.
Phone your Gram
and thank her.

Phone?
You know it's dangerous
to phone during storms.
I thought I heard . . .
Wasn't that thunder
a minute ago?

Phone?
I think that telephone cord
is way too long.
A person could strangle
getting tangled in that
couldn't they?

Phone?
Did you read the story
about a boy
who was kidnapped by aliens?
They sucked him
right into the phone.

Phone?
But I might dial a wrong number
and wake someone up
You know my memory
and my arithmetic are not great.

Phone?
What if Grandma's
in the tub
or having a nap
or just on her way out.
I'd hate to bother her.

Phone?
All right
All right
I'll do it.
First thing tomorrow.

TURN UP THE SOUND

Many poets do not write their poems in limericks or couplets or acrostics or other forms. They write their poems in open verse. In open verse the poem takes its shape as the ideas take shape.

An important part of the shape of an open verse poem is the way we speak. Sometimes we say a lot all in one breath. I have done that when I'm in a rush:

> Have you got your lunch money don't forget to put out the garbage and remember I'll be a half hour later tonight.

Other times it seems as if a sentence takes many breaths:

> Matthew!
> How many times
> have I asked you
> to PLEASE
> put out the GARBAGE!

When we are telling a story we start speaking one way and finish another. Try saying:

> Once upon a time.

Now say:

> And they all lived happily ever after.

One person may speak one way, another person very differently. When you phone someone you can often tell which person at that house has answered before a name is given. Not always. My children do sound a bit like me and a bit like their father. See how many ways you can write hello to show the different ways people may say it. Use capitals, small letters, spaces, punctuation marks and so on to show differences.

Anyway, voices are interesting to play with in poems. Look at the poem *Harmonica Howls*. It is almost like a tiny play with the words that the sisters say, some actions and also what one sister is thinking. The poem's stanzas depend on what each person says. One stanza is four words:

> Let ME play it.

Another, twelve:

> TOO BAD
> Besides
> I don't want YOUR germs all over MY harmonica.

The lines of the poem depend on how many breaths the speaker takes to say the stanza. The whining sister says her line in one breath. The harmonica owner pauses to think out her reasons.

Have fun with your audio buttons. With your writing you can turn the volume UP or down, you can go fastforward or take

your
    own
        sweet
            time.

3
Skunk Juice And Other Exploding Comparisons

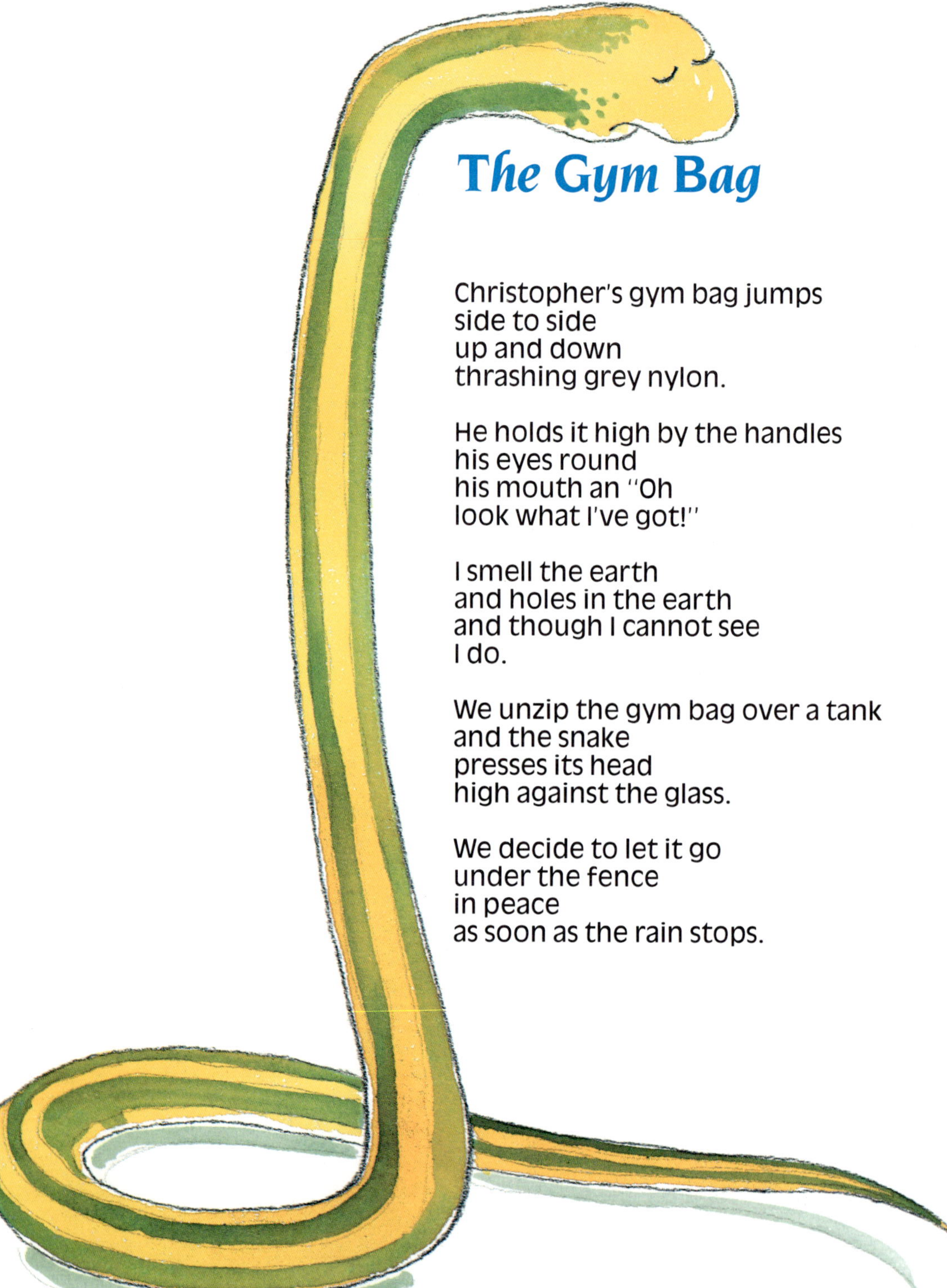

The Gym Bag

Christopher's gym bag jumps
side to side
up and down
thrashing grey nylon.

He holds it high by the handles
his eyes round
his mouth an "Oh
look what I've got!"

I smell the earth
and holes in the earth
and though I cannot see
I do.

We unzip the gym bag over a tank
and the snake
presses its head
high against the glass.

We decide to let it go
under the fence
in peace
as soon as the rain stops.

Skunk Juice

Help, Momma, help!

The kitty—
I didn't mean
to hit it with the stone.

Momma,
I didn't know
it would throw anything back.

Momma,
you wouldn't really
give me away?

Momma,
you're not really
going to bath me in tomato juice?

Momma,
is there anything else
I should know about skunks?

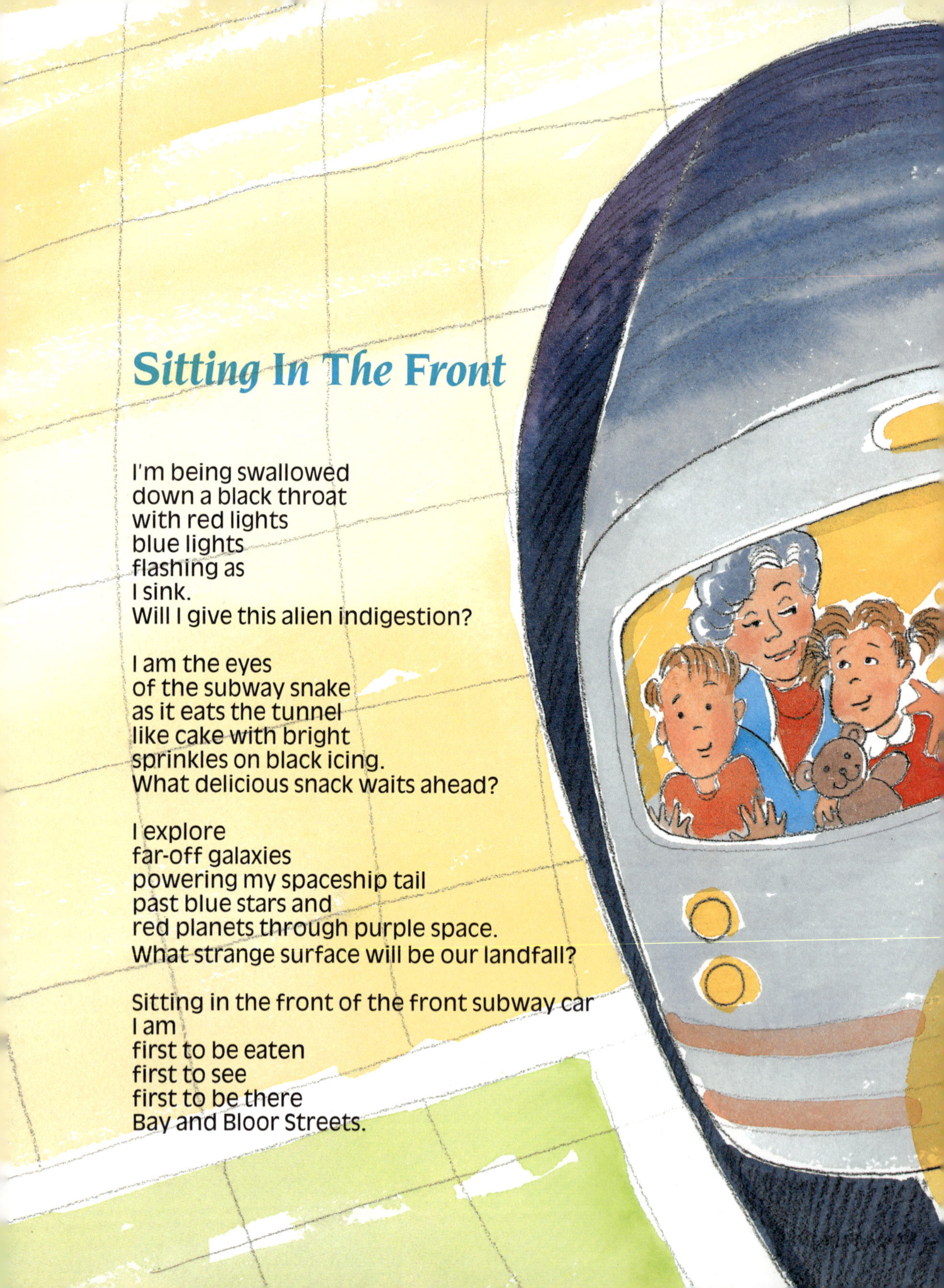

Sitting In The Front

I'm being swallowed
down a black throat
with red lights
blue lights
flashing as
I sink.
Will I give this alien indigestion?

I am the eyes
of the subway snake
as it eats the tunnel
like cake with bright
sprinkles on black icing.
What delicious snack waits ahead?

I explore
far-off galaxies
powering my spaceship tail
past blue stars and
red planets through purple space.
What strange surface will be our landfall?

Sitting in the front of the front subway car
I am
first to be eaten
first to see
first to be there
Bay and Bloor Streets.

Hugs

My teddy bear's EAR
is raggy because I chew it
when I'm scared of the dark.

My grandmother tells me not to
yell or slam the door because
it hurts her EARS to hear it.

My teddy bear's one LEG
came off and is sewn back
with black thread.

My grandmother has a
white scar on her LEG from
falling skating when she was a kid.

My teddy bear's EYE
is a button because
the brown glass one fell out.

My grandmother has new glasses
because her EYEsight isn't
what it used to be.

Bears are always there
but Grandmas hug back.

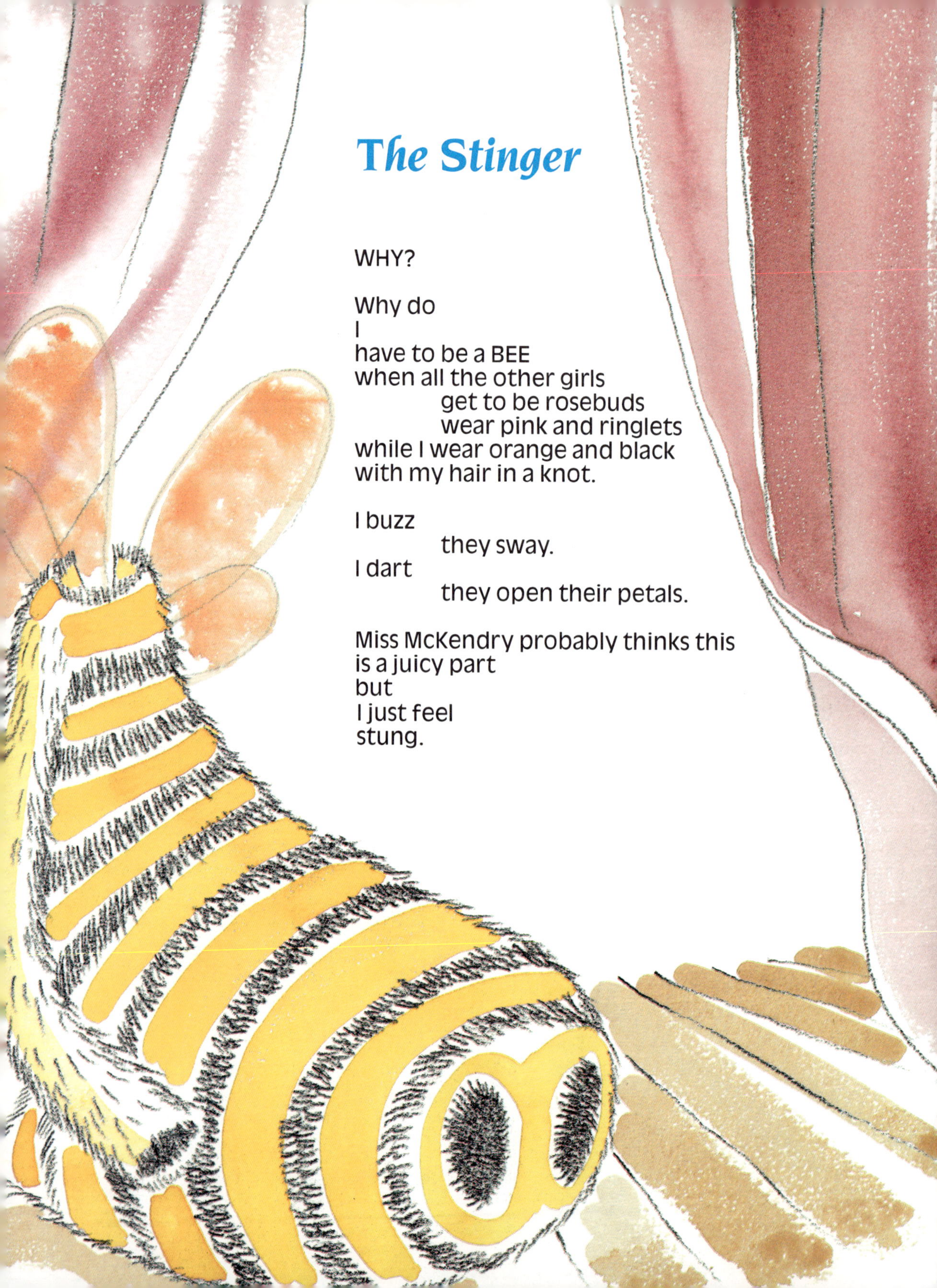

The Stinger

WHY?

Why do
I
have to be a BEE
when all the other girls
        get to be rosebuds
        wear pink and ringlets
while I wear orange and black
with my hair in a knot.

I buzz
        they sway.
I dart
        they open their petals.

Miss McKendry probably thinks this
is a juicy part
but
I just feel
stung.

Mount Crash

Oh, my knee is a map
of my stumblebum life.
Each scar is where
X marks the spot.

There is the place
where I fell off my bike
and there's the mark
of my best friend's cat.

There's the track
of the sidewalk I rollerskate
and the sign
of the library steps.

Oh, my knee is a map
of my stumblebum life.
and each scar is where
X marks the spot.

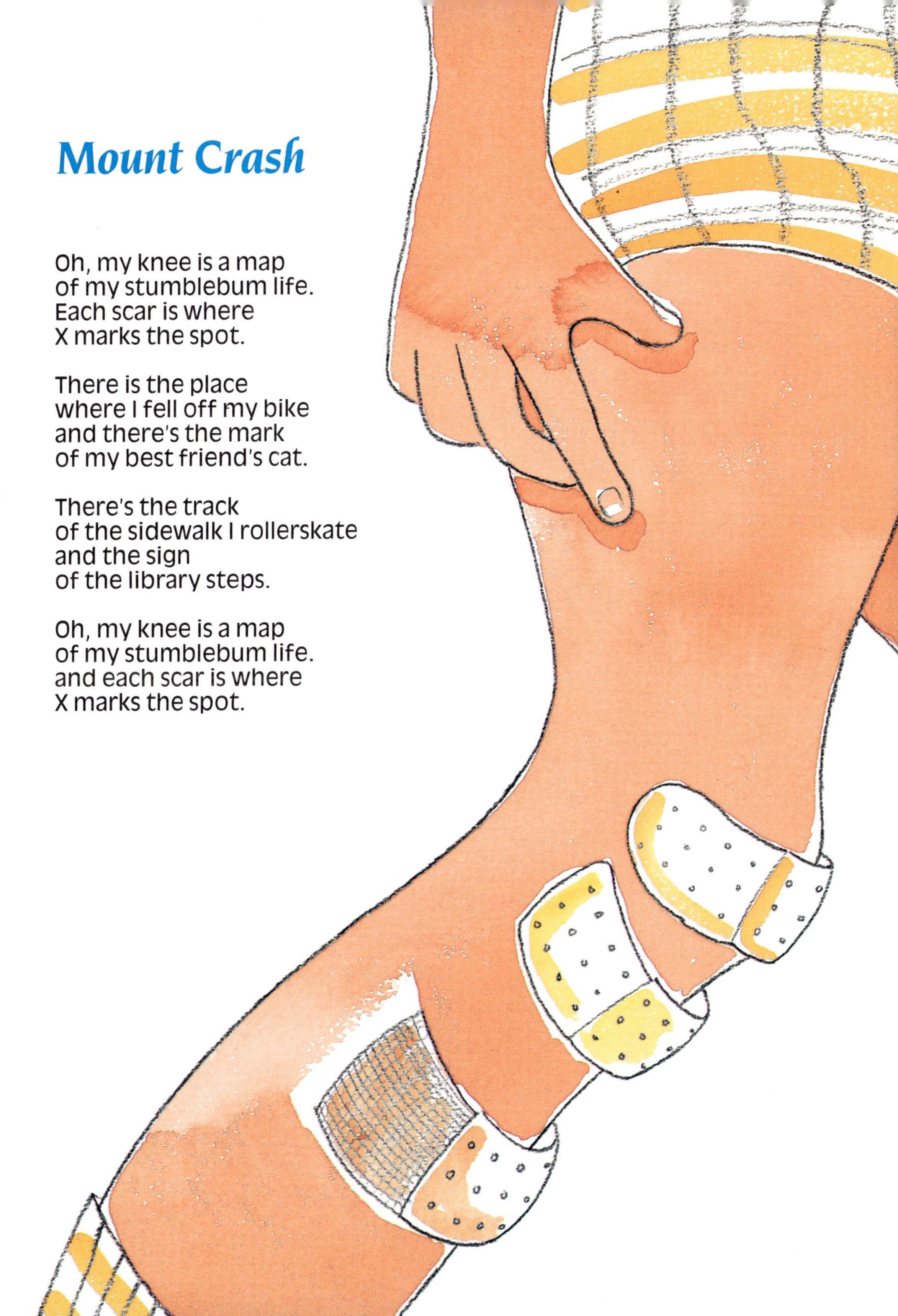

Home Wrestling Federation

In this corner
weighing two pounds and defending
the short-hair, tortoise-shell
Kitten Belt is
SPITTIN' KITTEN!

"ARRIVA, BABY!"

In this corner
weighing two ounces and defending
the hand-knit, blue wool
Argyle Belt are
ROCKO AND SOCKSO!

"MACHO, MAN!"

And here are a few words from our champ
"I'm fast and I'm sharp
and I'll whip them
against the ropes
even if there are two.
Nip their heels.
Stomp on their toes
and hold them down for the count.
No way they're
walking away from these paws.
Socks are wimps.
Cats are winners!"

And that's just what's happening, folks!

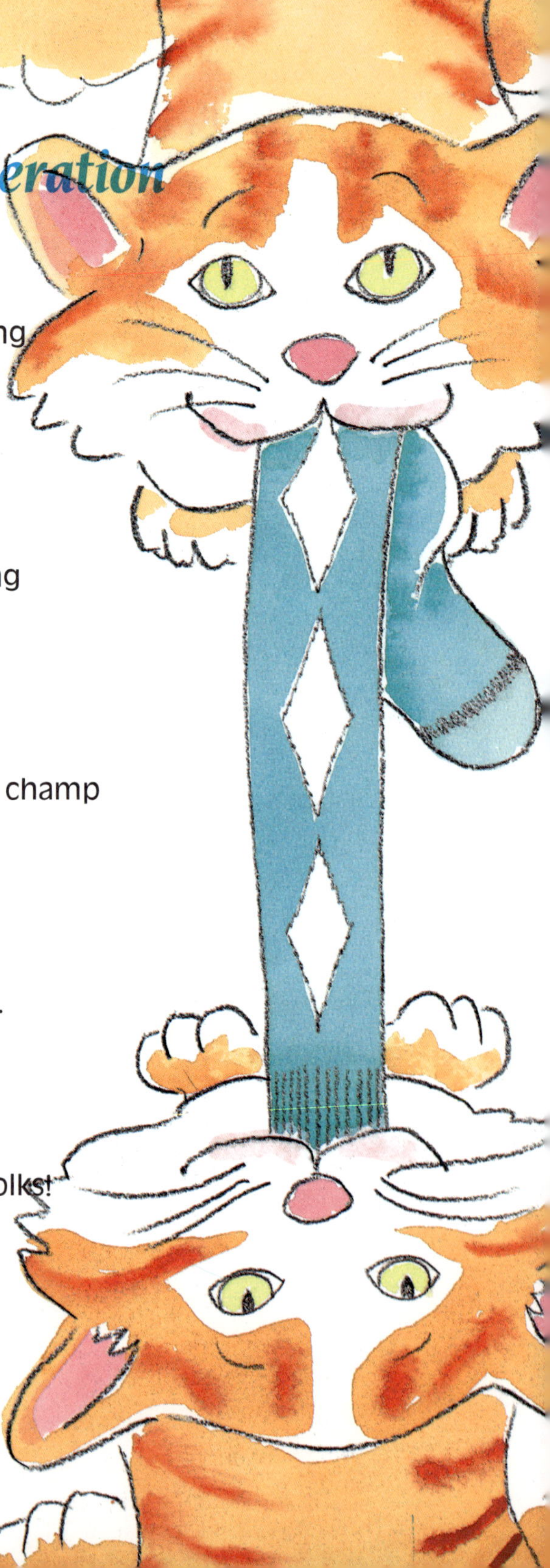

My Underwear's Inside Out

Oh, my underwear's inside out.
It's just been one of those days
and my shirt is buttoned up wrong.
I could tell when I tucked sideways.
My zipper got stuck
though I tugged and I pulled
and my rainboots have a hole.

Quit looking as if you know how it feels
to have ridges over your hips.
You couldn't possible understand
one collar tickling your chin.
Your finger doesn't have zipper tracks
nor your toebones icicle nails.

You'll never know how uncomfy I am
unless
(Can it be?) Is it true
your underwear's
inside out too?

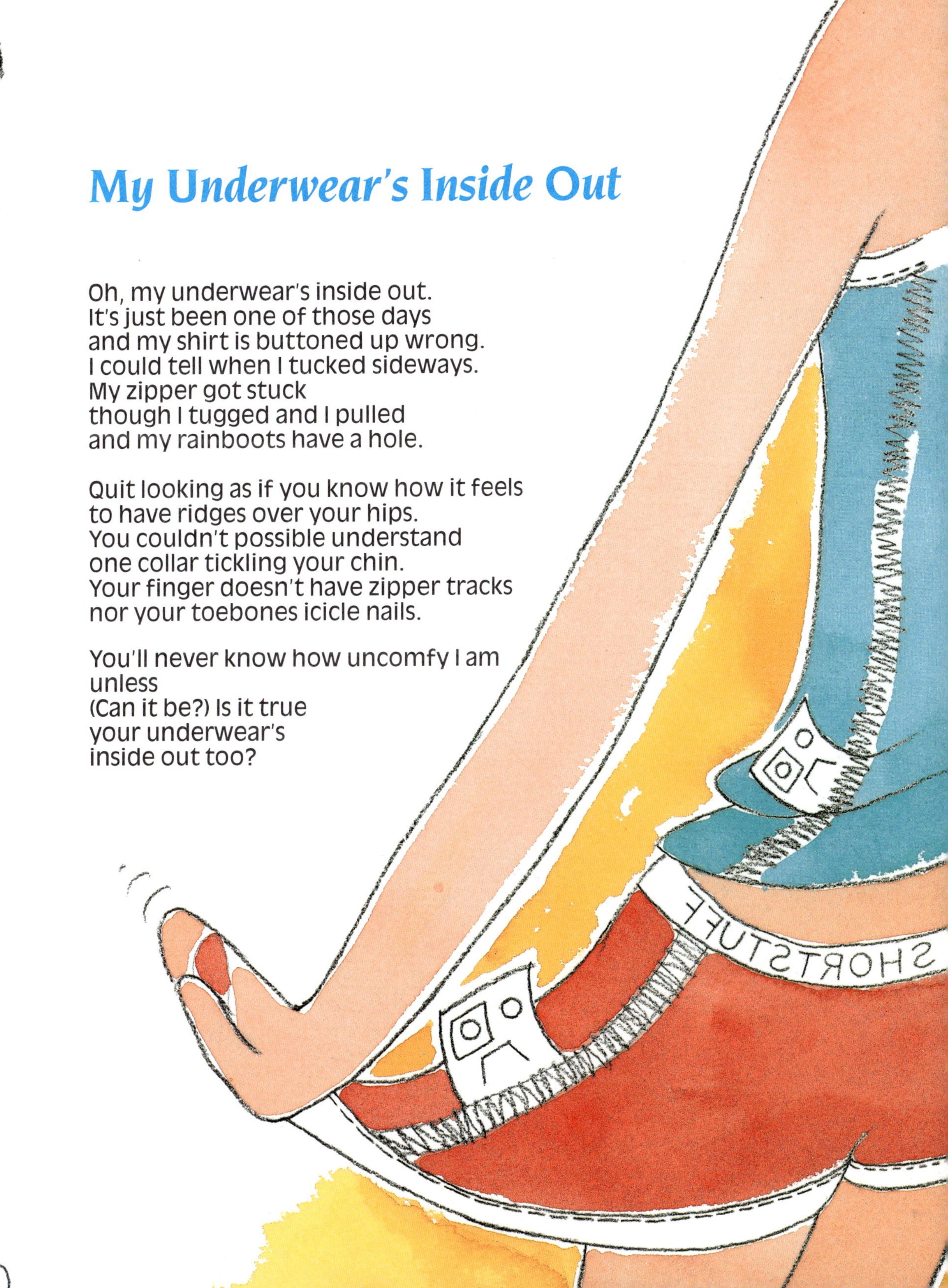

EXPLODING COMPARISONS

Many people have a habit of comparing. "You're just like your brother," someone will say. Or, "That leaf is just like a rabbit's ear." Comparing seems to be human nature.

Writers use comparisons a lot. Often the writer will talk about the ways things are the same. "She had hair the color of a maple leaf in the fall." "The baby's hair was soft as cat's fur."

You can have a lot of fun by looking at not only the ways things are the same but also the way things are different. Comparing situations is fun too.

A young friend of mine told me that he had once been sprayed by a skunk. I had never heard of a person being sprayed but I did have cats who had been sprayed. I knew what I would do to the cats. I would feel like locking them out but I would give them a bath in tomato juice. I asked my friend what his mother did when he got home covered in skunk spray. Sure enough she was upset but she took him in and gave him a bath in tomato juice. So the cat and my friend got the same treatment. The only difference was that my friend learned about skunks whereas my cat has been sprayed a number of times and doesn't seem to learn to keep away from them.

I remember my bent grandmother taking us downtown in Toronto where she lived. She always thought it was a treat for us to be in the front car of the subway. I had mixed feelings. It was scary and it was interesting and it was fun all at once. My poem called *Sitting in the Front* compares being in the subway to other things that might be scary and interesting and fun. The one thing that was different was that I knew that we would always end up at another subway platform but I didn't have to think that until the very last.

When I was writing this chapter, I was making lists from the poems of the similarities I found in things but I wanted to write about how exciting the differences could be. It made me think about the differences between Jason and my cat, between daydreams on the subway and the real subway ride. I went back and made some changes in my poems. I made some exciting discoveries.

When you think two things are alike, make a comparison chart like this:

Jason sprayed by skunk	Cat sprayed by skunk
skunk wins	skunk wins
talks / cries	mews / cries
stinks	stinks
cleaned up by Mom	cleaned up by me
bath in tomato juice	bath in tomato juice

Now add some differences.

learns to leave skunks alone	doesn't learn to leave skunks alone
wonders	doesn't wonder (Does he?)

Comparisons can make you think harder about your idea. You can make some interesting discoveries and find out what it is you don't know. Poets and other writers are like scientists in that they are always trying to find out things and wondering about things. Every poem is an experiment!

In an experiment you decide what will be a successful result. The only way to tell if a poem experiment worked is to read it to someone else and see if she or he understands what you are saying.

Be careful. I've known a poem to blow up in my face before!

4
The Floating Concrete Kraken And Other Magic Shapes

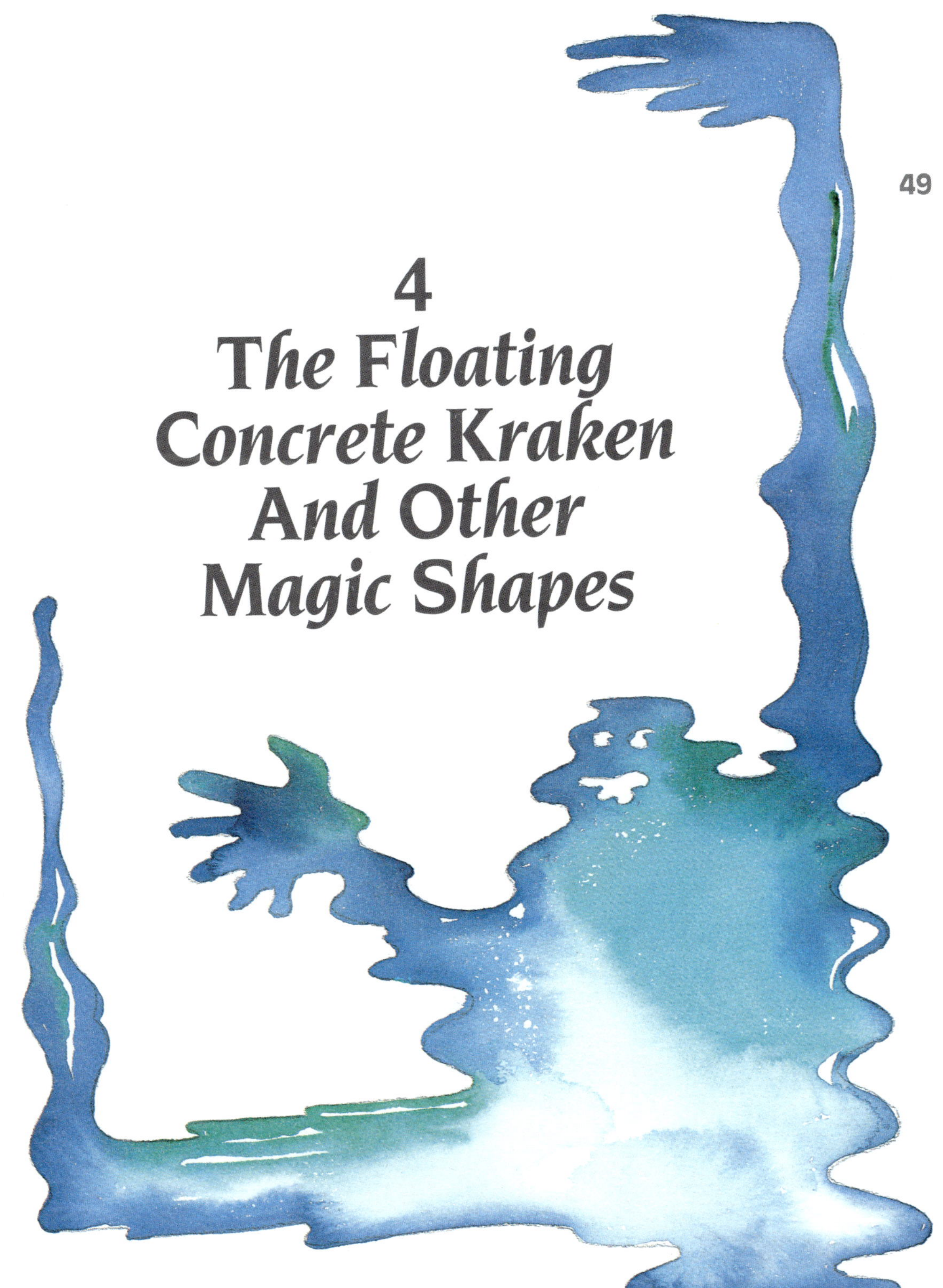

Floating Concrete Kraken

walkin' the greeny dark bottom of the sea.

talkin' the swishy roaring language of the sea.

stalkin' the floating frightened victims of the sea.

mockin' the flimsy cockleshell sea sailing ships.

The Ballad Of The Mermaid

The mermaid is a beautiful lass
but a fishy tail has she
and she lives not on the green green grass
but underneath the sea.

The pirate he is devil-may-care
and a small brave ship has he
but neither kin nor mere or pere
so he sails upon the sea.

Waves so high heave over her head
and they shake the deck to his tread.

The mermaid she is combing her hair
on a rocky islet shore
when who should spy her sunning there
but the navy's man of war.

"O look," they shout. "Her scales are gold."
And they're very fond of loot.
No nets they have but guns in their hold
so they creep alee and shoot.

Waves so high heave over her head
and they shake the deck to his tread.

And The Pirate

The pirate is a-listening
and he hears that deadly shot
so over the sea a-glistening
he goes without a thought.

To where the mermaid lies in pain
and he faces her enemy.
Then he fires at them again and again
and he makes the cowards flee.

Waves so high heave over her head
and they shake the deck to his tread.

The mermaid sore is injured
but he nurses her tenderly
and when she is well he lets her go
back to her native sea.

After that there is never a storm
but his ship goes safely through
and when he dies they bury him
near the rocky islet too.

The waves so high heave over her head
and now over her pirate dead.

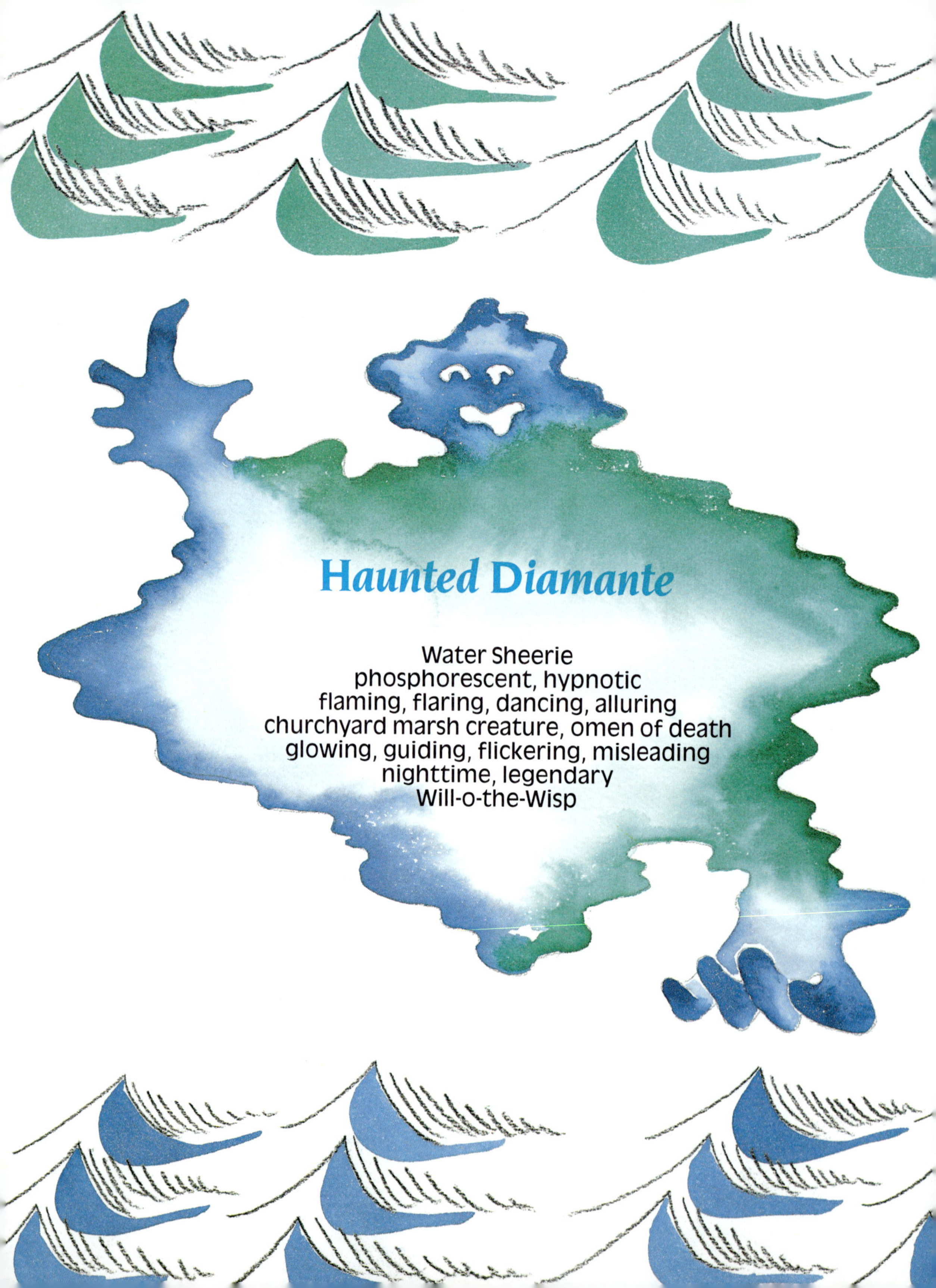

Haunted Diamante

Water Sheerie
phosphorescent, hypnotic
flaming, flaring, dancing, alluring
churchyard marsh creature, omen of death
glowing, guiding, flickering, misleading
nighttime, legendary
Will-o-the-Wisp

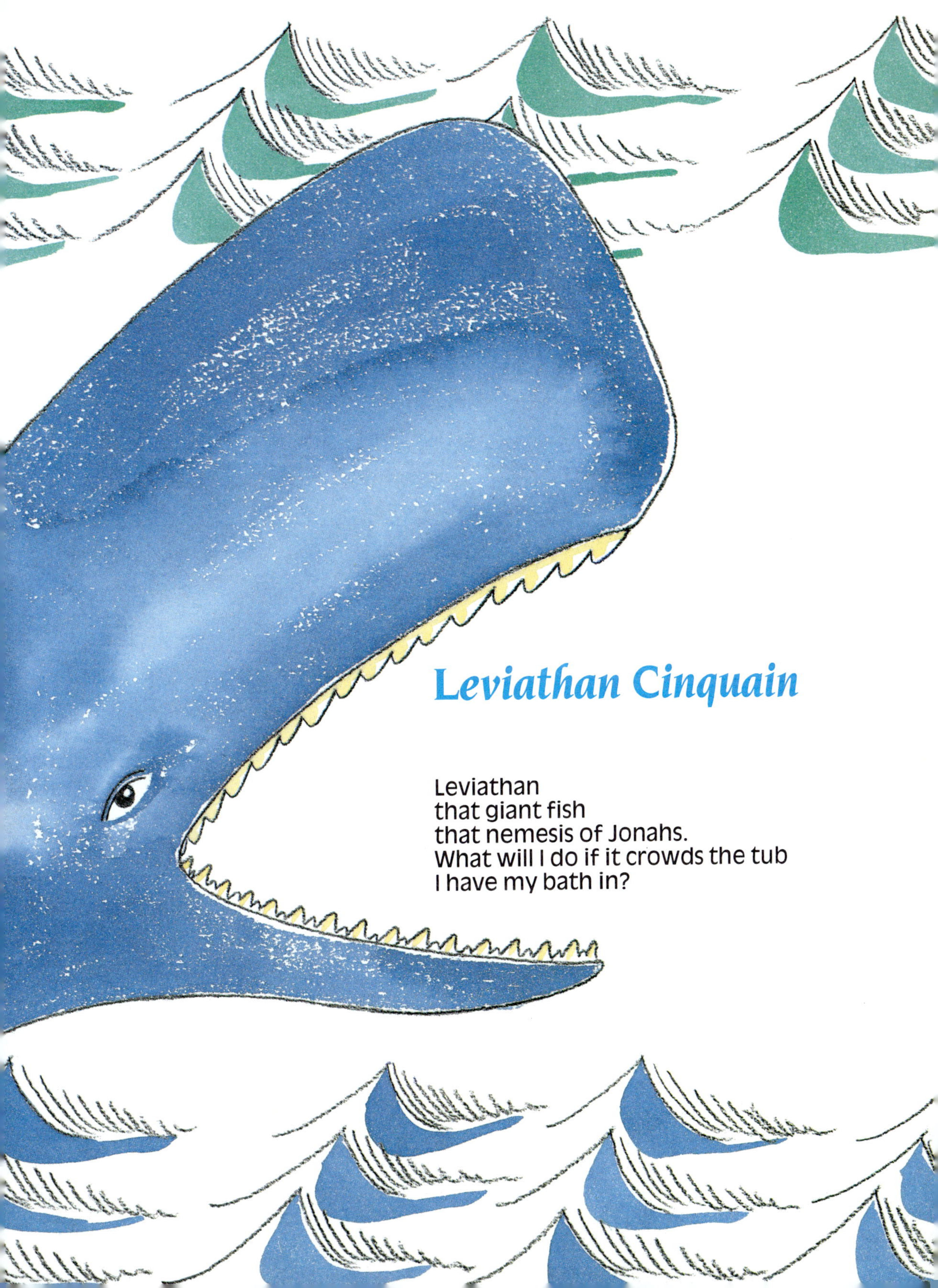

Leviathan Cinquain

Leviathan
that giant fish
that nemesis of Jonahs.
What will I do if it crowds the tub
I have my bath in?

The Reputations Of Sea Serpents

In Scotland's Ness
the sea serpent
has been researched
with thoroughness
but:
Och, brither
it'll eat you.

In Ireland's lake
the peistha beast
by Saint Molua
was given the shake
but:
Ay! Ay! freen
it'll eat you.

In Iceland's vatn
cold and clear
under midnight sun
the skirmsl fatten
and:
Vissulega, vinkona
it'll eat you.

There is a lau
in Africa
in Lake Victoria
it makes a row
so:
Ndiyo, rafiki
it'll eat you.

A Canadian fright
is the okopogo
that haunts Okanagan
and my dreams at night
and:
For sure, eh
it'll eat you.

In Lake Champlain
there's one called Champ
that more and more folks
have seen again
et:
Certainment, mon ami
it'll eat you.

Along the coast
of Chesapeake Bay
there swims the Chessie
some Americans boast
and:
Okay, pal
it'll eat you.

Around the earth
sea serpents curl
so your lake next
may give one birth
then:
Aye, matey
it'll eat you.

Scamphibian

There's a creature coming out of the sea.
Should we stay awhile and see
or should we flee
get ready for a fight
or satisfy our curiosity?

It's got spikes sticking up on its head.
They are brown and yellow, green and red.

It's got an eye as wide as all its face
that shines and glares. Oh is it saying grace?

It's got a sucking mouth that's long and blue.
I've a feeling it will stick to us like glue!

It's feet are black and wobbly, webbed and huge
with a body that is red, red as rouge.

Is it a monster from the sea?
Shucks, no.
It's only snorkel me.

MAGIC SHAPES

When you have an idea for a poem or any other kind of writing, it often helps to write down all the words you can think of which have to do with your idea. These words might be names, descriptions or actions. This word list helps you remember more about your idea and keeps you from leaving out important parts.

There are special kinds of word lists too. If you want to write your idea as a poem with rhymes or other word play, it helps to make a rhyming word list. To do this, take the first step. Make a list of words about your idea. Beside these words, write down other words that rhyme with them. Go through the alphabet for each one to check for rhyming words. I'll give you an example of what I did.

Even though I wanted to write a concrete poem about the kraken because of its interesting shape, I kept saying the word to myself. I liked the sound of it, so I made a list of rhyming words. One problem was that the word could be said two ways so I made two lists:

kraken—awaken, bacon, Jamaican, forsaken, shaken, windshaken, mistaken, overtaken, taken, undertaken, uptaken, waken

kraken—(for these words I had to make the slang form and drop the 'g') balkin', caulkin', dockin', flockin', gawkin', hawkin', lockin', mockin', knockin', rockin', stalkin', stockin', talkin', walkin'

Another help is a rhyming dictionary which will give you the endings of words and lists of words that end those ways.

The next step is to pick out the words which will help you say what you want about your idea. I chose "mockin'", "talkin'", "stalkin'", and "walkin'" because they seemed like things that the kracken might do under the sea and because the dropped 'g' seemed like fun. I looked at the kraken shape and decided that the head would be the first part of each line, and that a rhyming word could start every other tentacle.

Once you have a rhyming word list (and don't forget small words like "be"), then you can try them in the places where you need them and see if any make sense. Then write your lines to end with the words.

The important thing is to make sure your rhyming words make sense and are important to your idea. Never be satisfied with a rhyme that doesn't help your idea. If you are not satisfied, you can change to a different poem form.

A concrete poem is one that is written in the shape of something. When would you want to write a concrete poem?

If you make your word list and one of the words tells you about an interesting shape, that can be the time. For example, if you visit a bee keeper and are chased by bees, you might write a poem in the shape of a hive or a swarm.

If you see something you want to write about and it is an interesting shape, you can then too. For example, you visit an orchard and really enjoy the taste of fresh apples; you might then write an poem in the shape of an apple.

If you are interested in a certain topic and there is a shape associated with it, that's another time. For example, I was interested in mythical water creatures so I wrote about the kraken in its own shape.

The only problems to solve will be putting the words in that shape. Sometimes the shape is too complicated. Sometimes other people won't get it. Otherwise it is an interesting puzzle to solve.

A diamante poem is one with synonyms (words that mean the same) or antonyms (words that mean the opposite) at the top and bottom. When might you want to use a diamante (besides when your teacher tells you)?

I use a diamante when I notice something that has surprisingly opposite things about it or surprisingly similar things. For example, shadows in summer and winter or one person when young and old.

I might also use it when I find synonyms or antonyms in my word list about a topic. The only problem after that is to find the right number of interesting describing words, action words and naming words to fill up the lines. Use your word list, your thesaurus and your dictionary to help you.

A cinquain is a poem with five lines. There are many variations of a cinquain. My *Leviathan* poem is just one. The limerick is another famous one. I use this kind of poem when I have a very short idea to tell and a surprising ending. The main problem is to pack such a short poem with everything you want to tell.

When I have a long story to tell, then I might use a ballad. Ballads can be sung and often have repeated parts called refrains. I like them because they tell what happened to people and they often have the supernatural in them like ghosts and so on. The main problem is to keep on making many verses in the same pattern.

Whatever form of poem you try, it is like a puzzle, finding just the right words to fit the pattern, to make sense and sound interesting. What a pain it is to have a missing piece but take delight in searching for it. I hope your concrete poems float and your other poem tricks work.

Afterword

62 So now you've read my poems together with your child and maybe you've even tried to write one or two yourself. What's next? Well, you can supply buckets of tender listening care for the sands of experience and the waves of words your child will mix to make a poem.

Caring for the needs of younger poets at home or in the classroom is not easy. But you can start by praising the first steps your child takes in writing a poem and then pick out for special attention some part of the poem that is unique, insightful, or true to the child's voice. Sometimes this can be a touchy job but you can be sure that praise will encourage another effort and that the new poem will build on the strengths you have admired. Keep building strength upon strength and your child will craft many poems to be treasured.

Have fun on the beach!

Diane Dawber

Index of Titles

The publisher acknowledges the assistance of The Canada Council and the Ontario Arts Council. The author acknowledges the assistance of the Federation of Women's Teachers' Associations of Ontario.

Canadian Cataloguing in Publication Data

Dawber, Diane, 1946–
My underwear's inside out

Poems.
ISBN 1-55082-010-9 (bound) – ISBN 1-55082-011-7 (pbk)

1. Children's poetry, Canadian (English).
2. Children's poetry. 3. Poetry—Authorship—
Juvenile literature. I. Title.

PS8557.A8468M9 1991 jC811′.54 C91-090143-0
PZ7.D39M9 1991

Designed by Keith Abraham.
Printed and bound in Canada by Hignell Printing Limited.

Distributed in Canada by Prentice-Hall Canada, 1870 Birchmount Road, Scarborough, Ontario M1P 2J7 and in The United States of America by Bookslinger, 2402 University Avenue West, #507, St. Paul, Minnesota 55114.

Published by Quarry Press, Inc., P.O. Box 1061, Kingston, Ontario K7L 4Y5 and P.O. Box 348, Clayton, New York 13624.